Maisie Digs Up The Past

Maisie Digs Up The Past

Author and illustrator Aileen Paterson

THE AMAISING PUBLISHING HOUSE LTD

GLOSSARY

boomerang	Australian aboriginal weapon
didgeridoo	Australian aboriginal musical instrument
nippy mince	chilli con carne
peely-wally	pale
dinky	petite
tablet	Scottish fudge
frazzled	worn out
flabbergasted	stunned
nifty	agile

I would like to thank Nardini's of Largs, my son Liam for his help on expeditions, and Wilma Nicol, Leven, and also Mark Collard, for answering my questions on archaeology.

This story is dedicated to Anne Lauchlan Stoddart, Sarnia, Ontario, who shared my past at Burntisland Primary School.

Sites include:
Claypotts Castle, Dundee
Earlshall Castle, Fife
Standing Stones, Lundin Links, Fife
Nardini's Cafe, Largs, Ayrshire
Pictish Stones, Meigle, Perthshire
A cinema, Lochgelly, Fife

© Aileen Paterson

First Published in 1994 by The Amaising Publishing House Ltd, reprinted 1997.

This edition published in 1999 by:
Glowworm Books Ltd, Unit 7, Greendykes Industrial Estate,
Broxburn, West Lothian, EH52 6PG, Scotland

Telephone: 01506-857570
Fax: 01506-858100
E-mail: admin@glowwormbooks.co.uk
URL: http://www.glowwormbooks.co.uk

ISBN 1 871512 41 7

Printed and bound by Scotprint, Musselburgh

Reprint Code   10   9   8   7   6   5   4   3

Maisie MacKenzie's Daddy is a fearless explorer cat who travels all over the world. While he's away, he sends lots of letters to Maisie, and when he comes home to Scotland, there are strange and exciting surprises in his suitcase.

Sometimes Granny finds the surprises a bit *too* strange. Once Daddy brought back a pet TARANTULA called Waldo. He was a humdinger – the biggest, hairiest, spider you ever saw. Granny took one look at Waldo and climbed on top of the wardrobe. She wouldn't come down until Daddy and Maisie took Waldo to stay at Edinburgh Zoo!

Once he brought Maisie a
boomerang and a didgeridoo
from Australia. When Maisie
practised throwing the
boomerang, it flew round the
sitting room, chopping the heads
off Granny's flowers and
knocking everything off the
mantelpiece. Granny said she
didn't care for boomerangs.

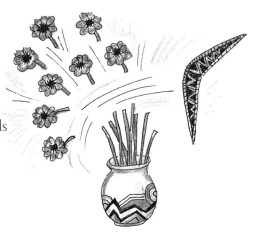

"Do you like my *didgeridoo*?" asked Maisie

"No, I didgeridon't," laughed Granny. "When you blow it, the
noise makes the walls shake. Mrs McKitty thought Edinburgh was
having an earthquake!"

Maisie loved all Daddy's presents, but she and Granny agreed
that the best thing Daddy brought home was himself. They were
both delighted when he arrived home on the first day of Maisie's
school holidays.

First of all there were lots of hugs, then lots more surprises
from Daddy's luggage.

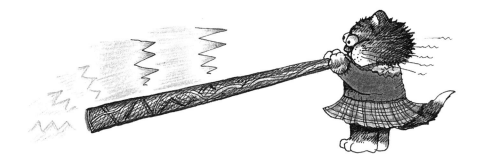

When Maisie's friends, Archie, Effie and Flora dropped in that afternoon, they thought Granny's flat had been invaded by Mexican bandits! There were Jumping Beans hopping about, and Maisie and Granny and their neighbour, Mrs McKitty, were dressed up in big sunhats called sombreros and stripey blankets called ponchos!

Little kittens are full of curiosity, and Maisie and her friends wanted to know all about Mexico. Daddy told them about his expedition, and showed them photographs of strange birds and animals. He said everything about Mexico was HOT, including the weather and the food. He said even the *mince* was nippy!

"Where are you going next, Professor MacKenzie?" asked Archie.

"It must be fun to go on expeditions," said Flora.

"It must be fun to eat 'nippy mince'," said little Effie.

Daddy said he wasn't planning any more expeditions for quite a while. He said he needed a rest, so he was going to take Maisie and Granny away for a quiet holiday in the country for a few weeks. Maisie clapped her paws and purred. It would be nice to have her Daddy stay at home for a long time.

"A few weeks in the country? What a good idea," cried Granny. "I could just do with a change from the traffic and the busy city."

"Exactly! A holiday in the country, far from the hurly-burly is just the ticket!" said Mrs McKitty. "*I* shall come too. I'm shattered to fragments after decorating my lounge and going to the sales – and my poor budgie is looking dreadfully peaky."

"We would like to come *too*!" cried Archie, Effie and Flora.

It was beginning to look as if Daddy's quiet holiday was turning into a major expedition . . .

"You are all welcome to come along," said Daddy smiling. "But I will have to come and speak to your mummies and daddies to see if it's alright, and tell them all about it. Mind you, the weather won't be as hot as it is in Mexico, and neither will the mince, if Granny is our cook!"

That evening he visited the kittens' families, and told them of his plans, and they all gave their permission. Next morning, Daddy booked a holiday on a farm, for three cats, four kittens and a budgie . . .

On Saturday, bright and early, the Morningside holidaymakers gathered on the pavement outside Granny's flat. Daddy loaded up his big new car with luggage and supplies. Rucksacks, suitcases, woolly jumpers, wellyboots, books, tins of beans, a football, porridge, tablet and budgie seed . . . then he helped his passengers on board and they were off!

Soon the busy city streets were left behind and they were driving along quiet roads with hedgerows full of red poppies and white daisies.   At last they drove down a winding lane and there, nestling amongst rolling hills, was Pitabootie Farm. In the field in front there was a caravan for Granny and Mrs McKitty and the kittens, and beside it, a tent for Daddy.

The kittens tumbled out onto the grass and began to play in the sunshine. While Granny helped Daddy to unload the car, Mrs McKitty took Billy the budgie with her to inspect their holiday home. She hung his cage by the open window and filled his water dish.

"Just sniff that fresh air Billy," she meowed. "A few days here, and you won't look so peely-wallie. What a delightful spot! Such a *dear* little caravan, such a dinky wee sink and cooker."

The farmer and his wife, Mr and Mrs MacTattie, came over to welcome them to Pitabootie. They brought some milk and butter, and an invitation to the kittens to lend a paw on the farm anytime they wished. That night, everyone went to sleep, comfy and cosy, thinking that Daddy's holiday plan had come up to scratch!

Next morning they awoke to a fine sunny day and the weather stayed fine. It was never so hot that any of the cats needed a Mexican sombrero, but no one needed a cardigan either. Some days they stayed at Pitabootie. Maisie enjoyed helping Farmer MacTattie with his cabbages, and riding on the tractor.

Granny cooked and sat out in the sun knitting. Daddy read books and Billy listened to Radio Tweet, while Mrs McKitty polished everything in sight. The kittens played football in the field. All the sheep gathered at the fence to watch Archie's nifty paw-work, and see him whizzing goals past Daddy.

The kittens fed the chickens and collected the eggs for Mrs MacTattie. Sometimes they were allowed to milk Peggy the cow and take the milk home for their porridge.

There were other days when they went exploring. Once Daddy took them all as far as LOCHGELLY for a curry dinner so that Effie could try some "nippy mince." She *loved* it, and kept cleaning her whiskers all the way home.

One weekend they visited a Fair by the seaside. The kittens rode on all the round-abouts. Daddy rolled pennies and tried to win a coconut, and Granny and Mrs McKitty had their fortunes told. The  Fortune Teller told both of them they would soon become famous. They smiled all the way home.

"One never knows, do one?" said Mrs McKitty.

 One night at bedtime, Daddy told Maisie that he had another good idea for a day away exploring.

"I've been reading lots of books about the history of Pitabootie," he said, "and tomorrow I'm going to take all of you to visit some of the local castles and ancient ruins. Won't that be fun!" Maisie made a face . . .

"Crumbs! *Castles and ancient ruins!* . . . that won't be very interesting. Can't we go to the Fair again? You know, Daddy, when Meeno the Space Kitten came to Scotland, he told me they don't like old things like that on Pluto. He said Edinburgh Castle was *so* old and dirty that we ought to knock it down and build a nice new one!"

Daddy laughed.

"What a daft idea! Castles are interesting because they are so old! It's time you learned about the past Maisie."

"But I know about the past," she cried, "Granny told me all about it. She said nobody had a fridge or a television set, and there were trams instead of buses, and Mary Queen of Cats got her head chopped off!"

But Daddy just laughed again, and kissed her goodnight, and said he was sure that tomorrow she would get a surprise.

There was a surprise waiting for *everyone* when they awoke next day, but it wasn't a nice one.

THE WEATHER HAD CHANGED!

A chill wind was blowing and rain was pouring down. It was so miserable that Daddy cancelled the trip to see the castles and they stayed indoors.

"Cheer up," cried Granny, "it might clear up by tomorrow. I'll make scones, and we can have a game of Snap."

But the rain didn't clear up. It poured for days. The kittens grew restless, and even Granny began to feel fed up, looking out at the view from the window.

"Dearie me," she sighed, "there's nothing as gloomy as a wet sheep."

Mrs McKitty changed her mind about the caravan now that there was a sea of mud outside, and too many cats and kittens inside.

"I'm absolutely frazzled," she declared. "This place is no bigger than a *treacle tin*. There's hardly room to swing a mouse."

Billy the budgie rang his bell and began to sing, "There's no place like home . . ."

Daddy looked at the muddy field and his soggy tent and the soggy sheep. The sky was full of dark clouds and the rain was still pouring down.

"Billy has the right idea," he said. "We'll pack up and leave for home tomorrow."

Archie, Effie, Flora and Maisie felt sorry to be leaving. It had been a wonderful holiday till the rain spoiled it. They put on their raincoats and wellyboots and set out for a walk and a last goodbye to Pitabootie.

"Mind and keep tidy now," cried Granny.

"And remember to wipe your paws on the mat when you come back!" cried Mrs McKitty.

The kittens crossed the field and began to climb the hill behind the farm. They clambered up in single file, the rain driving into their faces, the ground slippy beneath their boots. On top of the hill they paused and looked down. The farmhouse and the caravan looked tiny, and the cows and sheep looked like toys.

"Look," said Archie, "there's Farmer MacTattie putting his tractor in the shed. Can you see him, Maisie? MAISIE?"

There was no reply . . .

Archie looked around – Maisie *wasn't THERE* . . .

"Where has Maisie gone?" he asked the others.

They looked puzzled.

"I don't know," said Flora. "She was with us a minute ago."

"Well, she's not here now," said Effie. "I've counted us and we add up to three."

Feeling worried, they retraced their steps, scrambling down the hill shouting Maisie's name. There was no sign of her anywhere. Then, above the wail of the wind, came a loud meow . . .

They followed the noise . . . and found Maisie sitting at the bottom of a big muddy hole. The rain had washed away a bit of the hillside and Maisie had tumbled in!

"Are you alright?" asked Archie anxiously.

"I'm fine! I'm a wee bit muddy, but never mind about that. I've found something in this hole! I wonder if it's treasure?"

Sure enough, when the kittens took a closer look, they saw what Maisie meant. There was something shiny sticking out of the mud. They all dived into the hole and began digging excitedly with their claws . . . !

"Won't everyone be pleased when they see what we've found!" said Maisie, as they hurried home with their finds.

Mrs McKitty was not at all pleased. She was FLABBERGASTED when she opened the caravan door and saw the four mudcaked kittens. She wouldn't listen to a word about their "treasure", and she wouldn't let them in till there was newspaper all over her clean floor. Granny made them put all their muddy finds in a pail.

"Oh Maisie," she wailed, "I told you to keep TIDY. Even your ears are full of mud . . . you could grow potatoes in them!"

All four kittens were put, one by one, into the dinky sink and scrubbed with the sponge till they were clean again.

What with getting washed, dried, brushed and dressed in clean clothes,

the kittens couldn't get a word in edgeways about their treasure.
"Treasure indeed!" sniffed Mrs McKitty. "It looks like bits of old
bicycle to me."

When Daddy appeared at teatime, the kittens rushed to tell him
about Maisie's tumble into the hole in the hill, and they showed
him what they had found there.

Daddy lifted all the things out of the pail, washed and dried
them carefully and laid them on the table. Granny and Mrs
McKitty were astonished. These things were certainly not bits of
old bicycle . . .

There was a silver bowl and a heavy chain, cups and a
beautiful brooch.

THE KITTENS WERE RIGHT.
THEY REALLY HAD FOUND TREASURE! ! !

"What *are* these things?" asked Archie.

"What should we do with them now?" asked Flora.

"Can we keep them?" asked Maisie.

"You are very clever kittens," said Daddy. "You've brought home something very precious. These lovely things were made about a thousand years ago by the cats who used to live here. They were called the PICTS and the silver chain must have belonged to one of their kings. (The kittens were thrilled when they heard THAT!) Did you know that many of the places in Scotland whose names begin with PIT, like Pitabootie, were places where Picts once lived? I'm afraid that you can't keep your treasure. It belongs to every cat in Scotland. We'll have to phone the museum and tell them what you've done."

"What HAVE we done?" asked Effie.

"YOU'VE DUG UP THE PAST!"

After that lots of exciting things happened . . .

First of all the rainclouds blew away, so nobody wanted to go home after all. The Museum cats came to collect the treasure and dig up more of Pitabootie Hill, and that made the kittens feel very important. All the newspapers sent reporters to tell their story, and put their pictures on the front page, which made them feel even more important. Granny and Mrs McKitty gave interviews and became famous for a wee while, just as the fortune-teller had said!

Maisie told Daddy that she had changed her mind about finding out about the Past, now that she had seen a bit of it, so they all went exploring to find some more. Some days they went to see castles and learned about life five hundred years ago . . .

Sometimes they went to look at huge Standing Stones which were very mysterious because the cats who had put them there had lived *four thousand* years ago, and even Daddy wasn't quite sure what the stones meant . . .

But Maisie liked best of all when they went to see the stones carved by the Pictish cats whose silver treasure they had found. She thought they must have been very clever. The stones were covered in strange beasties and wiggly designs. And all the time they were exploring Daddy told them more and more about life long ago.

At night, when the other kittens were asleep, Maisie sat up thinking about it all. The past was really very interesting she thought. Why – Scotland was getting invaded every five minutes it seemed. She lay in bed and tried to imagine it all . . .

    Cats living in caves in Kirkcaldy and woolly elephants parading along Princes Street.

    . . . And no wonder the Picts got annoyed when the Romans marched into Scotland and started building walls and bossing everybody about! Then, as soon as the Romans had gone home, up sailed the Vikings. They must have been wild cats, always fighting and robbing . . . Daddy said the Scottish cats had beaten them in a big battle in Largs . . . maybe the Vikings had come to raid the Ice-Cream Parlour!

Daddy said that when the kittens got home to Edinburgh he would take them to the Museum to see their treasure on display. That gave Maisie an idea. She must tell Archie about it in the morning . . . Each of the kittens could put something from nowadays into a box, and they could bury it in the back green. Maybe one day some kittens from the future would dig it up and find out about them all.

What A GOOD IDEA!!
She snuggled down into
her covers and purred . . .
then she yawned . . .
and fell fast asleep!

I'm a little Pict, strong and brave,
My Granny and Grandpa lived in a cave,
I'm painted blue, and I've got a horse called Dave,
So if you see me riding by, give me a wave.

I'm a little Roman, short and stout,
I came to see what Scotland's all about,
The Picts don't like the Romans and they began to shout,
So we built a wall to keep them all out.

I'm a little Viking, I wear a funny hat,
I like to go on raids, I'm a bossy sort of cat,
I sailed my boat to Scotland,
Now I live here in a flat.

THE CHRONICLES OF MAISIE

I am Mary, Queen of Cats, you must have heard of me,
I am the most famous queen in Scottish history,
Before I lost my head, I used to do embroidery,
And visit lots of castles, and they let me in for free!

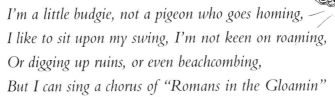

I'm a little budgie, not a pigeon who goes homing,
I like to sit upon my swing, I'm not keen on roaming,
Or digging up ruins, or even beachcombing,
But I can sing a chorus of "Romans in the Gloamin"

I'm a little kitten, Maisie is my name,
I'm noisy and nosy, and discovering's my game,
I've discovered Scotland's past, and the warriors who came,
But I'd rather live here nowadays, thanks all the same.